A
STROKE
OF LUCK

The Story & Experiences of a Stroke Victim

by
Bob Wragg

Published by Albion Press
54 Hollingdean Road,
Brighton, BN2 4AA

ISBN 978-1-9164418-1-1

Printed in Great Britain by
One Digital, Brighton

Introduction

This story describes some of my experiences during the six weeks I spent in Worthing Hospital following a stroke in 2022. The narrative is all factual – sometimes sad, sometimes funny but is not meant to be in any way a criticism of the Hospital in general or members of staff in particular. We all have our opinions of the N.H.S. in this day and age and I can honestly say that over the years, and particularly the last one, I have had excellent service and treatment. However I think I am entitled to my opinion if I feel things could have been done better or more professionally in certain areas. I have written it for three reasons, firstly as a 'thank you' to all my family, friends, and medical professionals in Worthing Hospital and the Community who have helped me during the past year, secondly as a therapeutic exercise and thirdly in the hope that it may help others who have also been unfortunate enough to have suffered a stroke and can perhaps relate to my experiences.

A STROKE OF LUCK

The Stroke

On Wednesday 9th March 2022 at the age of eighty I suffered a stroke which affected my left arm and leg and speech. It was sudden and unexpected. I have always been fairly fit for my age, playing sport when I was younger, although in 2004 I was diagnosed with skeletal stenos which required a major back operation and since then minor surgery. However I still suffer severe back pain which has curtailed some progress with the stroke.

I have been married for 58 years to a wonderful wife, Anne who was a qualified nurse for over thirty years, training at Hammersmith Hospital and working at several others. We have four wonderful children Steve, Andy, Chris and Tina, also five grand children and one great grand son. We had a daughter, Joanne, who died aged eight months in 1974. We have always been a close knit and loving family and have helped each other through usual traumas of life when faced with them.

In late April 2022 Anne went to visit Steve and his family in Florida He had recently had an operation for a detached retina. I did not go with her and stayed at home to look after our wonderful dog, a rescued Jack Russell named Finlay who I loved so much. Anne was due home on Monday 7th March. A few days prior to that Finlay became quite unwell with a bladder problem and on taking him to the vets I was devastated to be told he had inoperable bladder cancer and it would be the kindest thing was to euthanize him. I was desperately upset and contacted my daughter, Tina, who lives near us. She is an ex-veterinary nurse, she rang the vet and we both agreed with his advice. Tina was wonderful, she came with me to say goodbye to my little Fin and comforted me through the grief. We decided not to phone Anne with the sad news and ruin her holiday as she was due home in a few days. Four days later we met her at Gatwick Airport. We got in the car and she asked about Fin. I burst into tears and gave her the sad news. The house seemed so empty when we arrived home.

Wednesday 9th March started like any other. We got up at about 8am dressed and had breakfast. I don't remember too much after that but Anne recalls that she went into the garden to put out some washing and I was in the kitchen. I called to her for something, I'm not sure what, she came in and found me slumped over the draining board. "Bob, what are you doing, stand up?" My speech was evidently slurred and she helped me to a chair in the lounge.' I felt my left arm and leg were very weak with little feeling in them. "Bob you're having a stroke. I am phoning for an ambulance.' Anne said, her nursing experience obviously enabled her to recognise the symptoms. We did not have to wait long for the paramedics to arrive; they were very professional, took all my details and medical history and got me to Worthing Hospital very quickly where I was immediately admitted to Accident & Emergency Dept. I was examined by a Consultant fairly quickly and had a scan. Anne who had accompanied me in the ambulance stayed until it was confirmed I had suffered a stroke I was eventually transferred to what I was told was the Stroke Ward. It had ten beds all of which seemed to be occupied by male patients and it soon became clear to me that some of them were suffering from not only strokes but dementia and I think I was the youngest in the Ward.

On the first night I slept fairly well. The next afternoon I had quite a surprise. I had expected Anne and possibly my daughter Tina to visit. I was sleeping and woke up to see my sons Chris and Andy standing over Me.! The former who lives with his wife in Connecticut had immediately arranged leave from work and flown from the U.S. to the U.K. Andy, who lives with us had been on a motorcycle holiday in Europe immediately got a flight home from Seville, leaving his motorcycle there, in order to be at my bedside. I was so thankful to them not just for me but to support their Mum. Steve was unable to fly over because of his recent eye operation but he has been over several times since.

In Hospital

Shortly after that day sadly all visiting was cancelled due to a Covid outbreak in the Hospital but I can't express the love I felt for Anne and the kids visiting me when allowed, it really bucked me up.

The Nursing Staff, both full time and Auxiliary, Doctors, Cleaners etc. were of many nationalities, including English, Irish, Caribbean and Eastern European. Most spoke good English. The daily routine was much the same. Woken up at about 7am (no cup of tea, we had to wait until breakfast at 8am for that luxury)! Lunch was served at about 12 noon and dinner at 5,30pm I must say the hospital food was quite good. We were settled down for the night at about 9pm. I was unable to get out of bed unaided and had a daily bed wash also using a pee bottle and bed pan day and night when needed. Every couple of days I had visits from Physiotherapists and Occupational Therapists They would get me out of bed on a hoist to do exercises. I was told I should have daily physiotherapy but that was not possible due to shortage of Staff.)One Physio was good fun with a great sense of humour. Every time she came to see me she told me a joke and I had to reciprocate by telling her one. I won't repeat any of the jokes here though because the book may be censored ! The OT's job was to monitor my progress and, when the time came, make sure I had the appropriate equipment for my family to cope with me at home. To this end Anne and my son Andy attended two or three courses at the Hospital to learn how to lift me and use the hoist etc. During her nursing career Anne became a qualified Lifting and Handling Instructor and found it all quite familiar., Andy who had served in the S.A.S. also learnt very quickly.

It may sound strange to tell that for the whole six weeks I was in Hospital I did not speak to any other person other than Doctors, Nurses and Staff who dealt with me. I would describe myself as fairly gregarious although I do enjoy my own company at times. Soon after arriving on the ward it became obvious to me that several patients were not only stroke victims but suffered from other ailments, particularly dementia. I understand that due to old age that is often the case. Some just mumbled to themselves or talked incoherently. One patient who had or seemed to have some sort of business talked very loudly on the phone every night until quite late about work that he had to arrange for his staff the next day. Another talked to himself about sport, mainly football or footballers from past eras. There was a lot of shouting from some patients and I did find it difficult sleeping, in fact one night in the dim light I started to count the ceiling tiles! Apart from the stroke I suffered a lot of back pain I still do and it slows my progress with the former. Most nights I asked for Morphine in order to sleep. I was told that Morphine could not be prescribed for sleep but only for pain but when I explained my discomfort and inability to sleep, I was given it. The only problem was it made me very drowsy and I was often asleep when visitors came to see me. I have had Morphine in various forms since then but no longer as it sometimes makes me feel very sleepy and difficult to function, which is not good with a stroke. I just stick to taking Paracetamol and Ibuprofen.

An incident happened on the ward late one night for which I was admonished, probably rightly so (you decide)! One poor old fellow opposite me started shouting and succeeded in pulling down the curtains around his bed and rail holding them. This went on for several minutes, no help came and I decided to press my alarm button. After several more minutes the night nurse came straight to me, ignoring the patient opposite. "What do you want?" she asked. I pointed out the man opposite. "Oh don't worry about him, he's got dementia, and don't press your button if you don't want anything." She then went over and sorted out the poor distressed old boy. I fully understand that nurses work under great pressure but I feel the way that situation was dealt with was totally unprofessional and unsympathetic. My wife tells me that when she trained in the 1960's nursing was very much 'hands on, they learnt on the job and a Matron or at least a Sister would do a thorough and strict daily ward round often finding time to talk to patients. All the time I was in hospital I never saw a Sister on the ward except on two occasions when I asked to see her. Today I believe that registered nurses have to have a university degree before they can qualify. I wonder how much of their training includes the good old 'bedside manner?' The nurse's station was at the end of and outside our ward about twenty or thirty yards away with swing doors cutting off the view into it. It appeared that they were over-seeing three wards including ours', with a staff nurse responsible for each one.

I do want to emphasise that the nursing staff generally were very professional. However, my one main complaint was that I didn't feel the requirements of individual patients were prioritised enough, and there were many examples of that. On several occa-sions I asked for a pee-bottle or bed pan and was told to 'hang' on and one would be 'brought shortly.' That turned out to be several minutes and sometimes after a second request. On one occasion I actually soiled the bed! I saw other patients waiting to be fed with their food getting cold. What annoyed me about these incidents was that when a request was made and the patient was told they would be seen 'soon' and there was an unacceptable delay, the member of staff could often be seen doing other duties. When a patient makes a request surely it should be prioritised as to their needs.

Before I leave the subject of the Hospital and fellow patients I will address one subject that really annoyed me which I will call 'making promises and prioritising.' I experienced this several times and saw a number of other similar incidents with other patients, examples were asking for a bottle or bedpan and being told "Yes shortly." Often the request had to be repeated more than once and no indication or explanation was given for the delay. I appreciate Staff are always very busy, but even if a patient has a stroke or dementia a request made is usually important to them and should surely be prioritised if at all possible.

During my stay I became quite friendly with a Staff Nurse and we had several discussions about nursing, the state of the N.H.S. etc. I explained my concern about 'prioritising duties' and used an analogy which she was not too happy about, but it was the best I could think of at the time. It was as follows: -

Near to where we live is an excellent Fish & Chip Shop that does a home delivery service When a phone order is made the customer is told how long the delivery will take and that time is usually adhered to. If it is not the customer is contacted with an apology and a new time given. The food is always excellent and the shop staff, although busy are polite and helpful with any request. I related this example to my Staff Nurse friend and compared it to Nursing, especially not delivering a service for a request when told it will be and no apology or explanation if is not as to when it will be. Surely a request for a bedpan or help with feeding should be prioritised as much as possible but sadly I witnessed examples of this not happening which resulted in distressed patients. My friend did not appreciate my comparing the running of a Fish & Chip Shop with Nursing. Perhaps my analogy was not the best example and in no way did I mean to denigrate the work of the Staff Nurse, colleagues or their Profession I think she forgave me because she continued talking to me!

Everything was in place for my homecoming, the consultant was happy with my progress, a second scan showed no further bleeding on the brain and a couple of times he indicated that I should be ready to be discharged within a few days, however that did not happen. I was becoming more and more frustrated and my mental state was not good which was evident to Anne and Andy, especially when I was given the release date and it was cancelled the night before as I had tested positive for Covid! I was told it would be at least another ten days before I could go home. The family were not happy although they understood the reasons.

However, I was tested daily and after a few days I proved negative. I was given, I think, three different dates when I could go home but that did not happen The various reasons given included the Hospital not being able to arrange ambulance transport and the equipment needed at home had not yet been delivered. I was becoming more and more depressed and Anne contacted our G.P., an excellent Family Doctor of whom I will write about later (see acknowledgements). He agreed I would make better progress at home and suggested we should keep pressing for me to be discharged as soon as possible Eventually I was given a discharge date of Wednesday 6th April.

Going Home

Wednesday the 6th of April the day I had been looking forward to for about six weeks. I said goodbye to all the staff on the ward and the ambulance staff delivered me home at around 2pm where Anne and Andy were waiting to welcome me home. If it wasn't for various O.T.'s and Physiotherapists, especially since having the stroke I would never have been aware of what I was entitled to and could be funded by the various departments of West Sussex C.C. I wonder how many other stroke victims are not aware of their entitlements? My advice is just ask and keep asking. Since suffering my stroke I have had funding for a new central heating boiler as I had an unreliable one which could not be repaired or replaced. Also, I applied for my downstairs back room to be converted into a bedroom with toilet and shower. That was rejected due to the progress I am making, however, it was agreed that I should have a stair lift installed as it is too dangerous for Anne to help me get up and down stairs

When a patient is in hospital the total cost of all treatment etc is funded by the N.H.S. whereas on discharge any further treatment required, home equipment etc is funded by the local authority. While I was in hospital the physiotherapy and occupational departments were liaising with their counterparts who are employed by the various local authorities. They arranged to visit Anne at our house and get a hospital bed, a hoist, a commode, a zimmer and walking frame delivered for use when I was discharged. On getting into the house I was amazed at what preparation they had done in order to look after me. The back room had been converted into my bedroom with a hospital bed and a commode. There was also a hoist to enable me to be lifted and taken from room to room, also a zimmer frame. These had all been supplied by the occupational therapist and it didn't take long to get into a daily routine. Two carers came in at 9am each morning and 9pm each night, they got me out of bed, washed and dressed me each morning and then got me into bed at night and settled me down. The carers were not always the same two; they were supplied by an Agency and were very professional and good at their jobs. They were funded by the local authority but the funding only lasted for six weeks after which we were given the option of paying for the service if we wished. However during the time they were there Anne saw everything they did and she decided that she was quite capable of continuing what they were doing and it would have been very expensive for us to pay to continue with the Agency. In due course Anne coped brilliantly and in fact still does.

On the second day at home the Occupational Therapist and a Physiotherapist visited to ensure that everything was okay, they checked that Anne and Andy were able to help me on and off the hoist which they did without any problems. They also gave me a program of exercises to do daily. In addition Andy added to them with a strict regime which was much regimented. Having served in the army and the SAS he kept a close watch on my exercises in order to improve movement of my left arm and leg. Some people would describe his program for me as 'bullying', or in army parlance as 'beasting', however there is no doubt that without Andy I would not have made such rapid progress. He also had a great interest in my diet. One of my favourite foods is spam and he would not let me have it as he said processed meat was not good for me. However as I said earlier the OT's visited frequently during the early days and one particular one, Emma, when Andy was out one day, helped me get into the kitchen, sit on a perching stool and make a spam sandwich!

After a couple of weeks Steve having recovered from his eye operation, managed to fly over from the US which was brilliant. Prior to that Andy and Tina had managed to get me from my wheelchair into their cars and each took me out several times to Worthing seafront and the pier. When Steve arrived he also took me out for a coffee and a bite to eat in the town. Chris also came back over fairly shortly after I arrived home.

Steve, Andy, Chris and Tina, not to mention Anne, all managed to get me on and off the hoist and on the commode when needed. Indeed, I have awarded them all with the highly prized status of QAW (Qualified Arse Wiper) of which I'm sure they are very proud. As I pointed out I had carried out that service for them when they were babies and they were just returning the compliment.

An amusing incident occurred when my brother Geoff and his wife Pauline, who I hadn't seen for a couple of years, came to visit me from Ipswich. As they came through the door I was in the hoist hanging in mid air over the commode in a very embarrassing position with my 'crown jewels ' in view and they both just burst out laughing.

Luckily I did not have to use the hoist to get on the commode for too long as I gradually made good progress. Although I still had weakness down my left side I managed to get from room to room with the Zimmer. I even managed to master the thirteen stairs up to the bathroom with help. After the back operation I had in 2018 the Occupational Therapist arranged to have my bathroom converted into a wet room with a shower and seat as I was unable to climb in or out of the bath. She also arranged to have a handrail put on the right hand side of the stairs-there was already one on the left. She also had several hand rails put up in and outside the house- the latter have been a great help enabling me to get out to the garden All this was funded by the West Sussex Council to whom I am very grateful. If it wasn't for various O.T.'s and Physiotherapists ,especially since having the stroke I would never have been aware of what I was entitled to and could be funded by the various departments of West Sussex C.C. I wonder how many other stroke victims are not aware of their entitlements? My advice is just ask and keep asking. Since suffering my stroke I have had funding for a new central heating boiler as I had an unreliable one which could not be repaired or replaced. Also, I applied for my downstairs back room to be converted into a bedroom with toilet and shower. That was rejected due to the progress I am making, however, it was agreed that I should have a stair lift as it is too dangerous for Anne to help me up and down stairs. That has been installed and it is a great help enabling me to use the bathroom .Anne assists me to shower and we now have it 'off to a fine art' She is absolutely marvellous, caring for my needs, cooking, washing, doing the housework, shopping and managing her favourite task, gardening ,which she is very good at. She always keeps a beautiful garden of which she is so proud and there is nothing I like better than sitting outside admiring it and getting some fresh air.

Prior to me getting home Andy had returned to Spain to collect his motor cycle. He had also decided to give up his work as a H.G.V. driver travelling around Europe, which he loved, in order to stay at home and assist Anne in caring for me. I thought that was a wonderful loving thing to do for which I will always be grateful. Over the next months he obtained several jobs driving involving short local journeys, also one as Night Manager in an hotel in Brighton. He was never very far away in case Anne needed help with me. I am delighted that nearly a year on my progress has improved to the point that Anne copes with me so well that Andy has started a new driving job in Europe .

Mental Effect

There is no doubt that suffering a stroke does have a mental effect on a person. As far as I'm concerned it has done so in my case. The first thing I was aware of was jealousy and by that I mean seeing other people leading their lives as they wish and me not being able to. I even was jealous seeing people walking past the house and thinking "why can they do that and I can't". I have now realised the stupidity of having those thoughts and knowing that I have to accept what life has thrown at me. I reflect very much on my past life and regret not being able to do things that I used to enjoy such as playing rugby or cricket. I guess I could not have done any of that in old age anyway, stroke or no stroke, (although I had a friend who gave up playing rugby when he was seventy two!) I've now learnt to look back on my past life with happy memories and am even in touch with friends I grew up with sixty years ago. I've had to give up driving which restricts me a great deal. Just prior to the stroke I thoroughly enjoyed giving talks and lectures on cruise ships about my time as a detective in the Met Police in the 1960's. I took Anne with me at no cost. Also several months before the stroke I bought a mobility buggy and I used to take Fin out daily to the park. He would sit on the buggy between my legs and loved it. Unfortunately I had no use for it after the stroke and sold it. Shortly before the stroke I learnt to paint but now find it very difficult not being able to hold the palette in my left hand and paint with the right. Despite all this I feel I have come to terms with what I have and I appreciate other people far more than I did, thus, the title of the book "A stroke of luck" the luck of having many wonderful, loving people around me, including family, friends and medical professionals.

I have always been a sentimental person and have never been ashamed to show my emotions and cry. These feelings have now increased greatly One day Therapist, Emma, visited me at home to see what progress I was making. She told me I was doing brilliantly and my progress was "bloody amazing". I just burst out crying! If I managed to accomplish anything such as cooking , shaving for the first time after the stroke I would cry. It also happens a lot when I watch anything sad on TV, even the News and particularly seeing dogs. The latter I suppose is because I have not yet got over losing my little Fin. Also seeing someone achieve or succeed at something. I have discussed my emotional feelings with Emma and she says it is quite normal and probably good for me. Anne is sympathetic and calls me a 'silly old sausage'.

What Caused All This?

Anne and I always hate the month of March. We seem to have been cursed with the luck of Julius Caesar !

In March 1971 our beautiful baby Joanne died of pneumonia aged seven months. My Father, Mother and Aunt all died in March of various years. I am not superstitious and all that is coincidental, however, With losing Fin and my stroke happening in March we can't wait for that month to 'blow out'.

As mentioned above My Dad died quite suddenly in March 1965. He was the Chief Steward on a cruise ship, RMS Andes, and his Steward found him dead in the bath .The ship was in Antigua and he was taken ashore ,a post mortem carried out which showed he had suffered a massive stroke. Dad was buried on the Island and we had a headstone sent out for his grave. My Mum was never able to visit Antigua but my brother, sister and I have since been lucky enough to go and pay our respect to our Dad. I am not sure if it has yet been proved that strokes can be hereditary? Many reasons are given for the possible causes of strokes, in addition to the chemical changes in the brain such as stress, the latter of which I am sure contributed to my condition prior to it occurring, several traumatic events happened in my life which at the time and since which have effected me greatly. During the months before it happened my brother, Geoff, was diagnosed with liver cancer and underwent a serious operation . Anne's Brother Roy who had previously been diagnosed with cancer of the oesophagus and had earlier undergone a major operation from which he never really recovered. His health gradually deteriorated during 2002 which was worrying and he subsequently died shortly after my stroke. Two very good friends of mine also died within a short period of each other. Also as described earlier the week before I suffered the stroke I was forced to have my darling little dog, Finley put to sleep. My son Steve underwent a serious eye operation the result of which at the time we were unaware of the outcome. He seems to have now recovered, however, I am sure, as are my doctors, that these events might well have contributed to the cause of my stroke.

The Future

Obviously, and probably for the good, no one knows what the future holds for us. The general opinion is that I have and am making good progress and hopefully my prognosis is positive however, the one thing that does concern me , and of which I am fully aware, is that I could suffer another stroke at any time, or a serious fall. In fact I recently had one. I fell in the bathroom and hit my side against the toilet. Anne and Andy managed to pick me up but I think I broke a couple of ribs which were very painful for a few days. Also as mentioned earlier, I suffer from severe back pain which definitely hinders my stroke progress. My Consultant says there is nothing more can be done about that which I find most frustrating.

Such is life for anyone and I more or less live from day to day and accept my situation. If that were to happen I trust I will be able to accept and face the it with fortitude. I am generally a positive person (my blood group is B+). My glass I always half full not half empty. I never worry. Worrying about anything I have found does nobody any good, it just causes you to make bad decisions. Each morning I wake up, I think of and look forward to anything which I am going to enjoy that day whether it be sports that I'm going to watch on television, visitors who may be coming, or food that Anne is cooking. Each night before I go to sleep I reflect on good things that have happened that day e.g. Southampton winning a match, which is rare, being taken out in the car to Worthing or a shower I have had. I take great pride in seeing my family and especially my grandchildren achieve things in life. I am so looking forward to seeing my first great grandchild, Liam, in America sometime.   Yes, I do have several regrets. I used to love cooking but I have lost some of my taste. My food has to be cut up small for me and a Sunday Roast is just not the same all cut up when I see others tucking into large slices of roast beef! However, my daughter Tina bought a wonderful disability worktop for me for Christmas, which holds food when being prepared. Anne helps me and I do manage to cook a few things. I also get taken out for meals sometimes and I find the restaurants very obliging when we book and tell them I will be in a wheelchair.

My goal is to walk with a stick and do away with the zimmer but that is a little way off yet. I would like another dog to love and take for walks but Anne has far too much to do for me to expect her to get involved with that'. While I was in hospital I had several visits from the Speech Therapist as my speech had been affected by the stroke.. We agreed on several phrases that I should practice saying each day and they were (a) My name is Bob Wragg (b) I am sorry I can't answer the phone right now, please leave a message,(c) I would like s chicken madras please (d) I am a Southampton supporter. She encouraged me to read out loud when I got home and she checked on my progress a few times. My speech was quite bad at first. However everyone says it has improved but it is often slurred when I get tired. Also I often find it difficult to understand some people on the phone especially if they have an accent. I always explain that I have had a stroke and ask them to speak slowly Anne frequently has to take over the phone call for me, which is very frustrating.

I have been Southampton football supporter for many years and I have now got disability membership. In November 2022 when Steve came on a visit from USA he and Andy took me in the car to see a Saints match The club have excellent facilities for wheelchair supporters and we sat in the front row As I remember the team actually won that day. I do hope I will be able to repeat that great day out with the boys again sometime.

Yes, I have a great deal to be thankful for. I am not a religious person, but if there is a God or Greater Being I feel he has been and still is in my corner for which I am very grateful.

The End

Bob Wragg
February 2023

Acknowledgements

In writing this book, I hope that I might have helped other stroke victims. It has certainly been therapeutic for me. In doing so I wish to thank so many people, family friends and medical professionals and in other fields for their help and support who have helped me, many of whom I have mentioned in the narrative. I especially thank the following people and hope and apologise for any who I have omitted

My darling wife Anne ,my children Steve,Andy,Chris and Tina and their families' Christine my sister and her family, my brother Geoff and his wife, Pauline Also the many medical professionals including Nurses Physio and Occupational Therapists (Terrorists-their description, not mine!) and others at Worthing Hospital including Ward Cleaners, and Catering Staff. My Consultant Mr Sengupta. The Paramedics from the Ambulance service who got me to hospital so quickly The Home Carers, especially Maria and Richard.

The many Physio and Occupational Therapists and others who work for the West Sussex County Council Health Depts. especially Emma Parkin (O/T), Claire and Lucy (Physios) Shelley, Maria and Faye (Adult Care in the Community. Also thanks to Steve Dommett (Senior Environmental Health Officer, WSCC) who gave us so much help with paperwork which has resulted in obtaining a stair lift.

Many thanks to my great friends Lord Morrison (Morrie) and Ria for their constant support.

Antony Cawkwell and all who have contributed to the printing and design of the book at One-Digital.

Finally a very special thank you to our wonderful Doctor. Dr Sayers has been our Family Doctor for many, many years, He has a practice with one other doctor and he is without doubt the best G.P. one could ever wish for. He is professional, sympathetic and understanding and has helped me and my family through some very traumatic times.

Nothing is too much for him and we are able to arrange either phone and/or surgery appointments often within twenty four and certainly forty eight hours, which is very unusual these days. Since my stroke Dr Sayers has frequently been in touch with me or Anne to check on my progress and advise on prescription needs. He is an absolute credit to his profession.

About The Author

Bob Wragg was born in Wheathampstead, Hertfordshire, in 1941. He attended St Albans Grammar School and then King Edward VI School, Southampton

On leaving school he joined the British Antarctic Survey and served as a crew member on the R.R.S. John Biscoe for two years 1959 to 1961, visiting Montevideo, the Falkland Islands, South Georgia and Antarctica, travelling through the Weddell Sea to the British Base at Halley Bay, 800 miles from the South Pole- the first British ship to go there since Ernest Shackleton's Endurance in 1915.

On leaving the sea Bob joined the Metropolitan Police serving first in uniform in the east end of London and then in the CID in that area and then in south London and New Scotland Yard. On leaving the Police in 1973 he served as Security Officer with Cunard on the Cunard Princess and then the QE2.

On leaving that position in 1979 Bob spent several years as Chief Security Officer at various prestigious London Hotels and Retail Companies including F W. Woolworth, and HMV. He then became a writer and published author and prior to his stroke spent four years as a speaker on various cruise ships, clubs and societies.

Bob is married to Anne who spent 40 years as a registered nurse. They have three sons and a daughter, having lost one daughter when 8 months old.

Other books by the same author:

Jacob's Ladder
ISBN 978-09558103-3-6

The Secret War Diary Of A Worthing Soldier
ISBN 978-09558103-7-4

Bobby On The Beat (By Bob Dixon)
ISBN 978-1-78243-119-0